THE SESAME STREET PLAYERS PRESENT

The Little Red Hen

Starring:
BERT as the LITTLE RED HEN
And featuring:
ERNIE as the DOG · GROVER as the SHEEP
HERRY MONSTER as the PIG · COOKIE MONSTER as the COW
Directed by: PRAIRIE DAWN

Written by: EMILY PERL KINGSLEY · Illustrations by: TOM COOKE

Featuring Jim Henson's Sesame Street Muppets

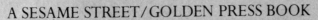

A SESAME STREET/GOLDEN PRESS BOOK
Published by Western Publishing Company, Inc.
in conjunction with Children's Television Workshop.

"Oh welcome, oh welcome to our little play.
We're ever so glad you could join us today.
Let's open the curtain. Our setting's a farm
So let's meet our star coming out of the barn."

"I am a chicken called Little Red Hen.
   One day I was wandering out of my pen
   When what should I spy, lying under a weed,
   But a bright shiny kernel...a beautiful seed!"

"So the Little Red Hen called her friends, small and big.
First a Dog…then a Cow…then a Sheep…then a Pig.

She told them a small bit of help she would need,
And asked, 'Who will help me to plant this fine seed?'"

"Not I," said the Dog. "I have bones I must dig."
"Not I," said the Sheep. "Why not try the Pig?"
"Not I," said the Pig. "I must roll in the mud!"
"Not I," said the Cow. "I'm still chewing my cud."

"Ah, forget it," said the Little Red Hen. "I'll plant it myself!"

"You friends wouldn't help plant the seed that I found,
So I did it myself. Now it's safe in the ground.
But dirt isn't all that a small plant will need.
So now who will help me to water the seed?"

"Not I," said the Sheep. "My wool I must comb."
"Not I," said the Cow. "I am writing a poem."
"Not I," said the Dog, as he frolicked and played.
The Pig said, "I'd rather go lie in the shade!"

"The Little Red Hen weeded, watered and all,
And in time the small plant grew up sturdy and tall.
Then she came to her farm friends quite early one morn
And said, 'Who will help me to harvest the corn?'"

"Not I," said the Pig. "It is time for my swim."
"Not I," said the Dog. "I'll be swimming with him."
"Not I," said the Sheep, "though I'd love to say yes.
   I am meeting the Cow. We've a date to play chess!"

"So the Little Red Hen picked the corn by herself.
Then she got down her grinder from the top of the shelf.
Said Hen to her friends, 'I hope you won't mind
Pitching right in and helping to grind.'"

"Not I," said the Sheep. "I am off to a show."
"Not I," said the Dog. "I have bubbles to blow."
"Not I," said the Pig. "I am riding my swing."
"Not I," said the Cow. "Grinding corn's not my thing!"

"So the Little Red Hen ground the corn into flour.
She beat in some eggs. It took over an hour.
Then she said to her friends, 'Well, you didn't help make them,
But these are corn muffins. Now who'll help me bake them?'"

"Not I," said the Cow. "My flies I am swishing."
"Not I," said the Dog. "I am off to go fishing."
"Not I," said the Pig. "In the sand I am rolling."
"Not I," said the Sheep. "It's my day to go bowling!"

"My muffins are baked now! They're hot and delicious!
They're made of my corn, which is good and nutritious.
You didn't help plant them or grind them or beat them —
But now that they're finished, who'll help me *eat* them?"

"I will," said the Dog. "Those muffins smell neat!"
"I will," said the Pig. "I'm ready to eat."
"I will," said the Cow. At the table she sat.
  The Sheep said, "I'm *never* too busy for *that*!"

"Now hold it," said Hen in her angriest tone.
"I planted and nurtured and baked all alone.
  You all were too busy to help, so you see,
  These lovely corn muffins will be eaten by... ME!!"

"Then the Dog and the Pig and the Cow and the Sheep
Were so disappointed they wanted to weep."

"The moral of our story is easy to see:
'If I help you, then you ought to help me!'
When friends help each other, that's a much better way.
And that is the end of today's little play!"

"Thanks, everybody," said Prairie Dawn after the play was over. "You were all very good. But listen, before we eat up these corn muffins, who'll help me put the scenery and the costumes and the make-up away?"

"Not I," said Ernie. "I have to go to my juggling lesson."

"Not I," said Herry. "I have to buy my pet canary a new pair of sneakers."

"Not I," said Cookie Monster. "Me have to go put Teddy Bear down for his nap."

Grover said, "I think I hear my mommy calling me."

"Hey, you guys," said Prairie Dawn, "didn't you learn *anything* from today's play?"

"Oh, Prairie Dawn," said Ernie, "we were only kidding! Of course we'll help."

And so Ernie and Grover and Bert and Herry and Cookie and Prairie Dawn put away all the scenery and costumes and make-up, and ate up all the corn muffins.